ROBERT HENNEBERGER

RED MULE

WHITTLESEY HOUSE

McGraw-Hill Book Company, Inc.

NEW YORK   TORONTO   LONDON

RED MULE

JESSE STUART

Illustrated by ROBERT HENNEBERGER

Also by Jesse Stuart
A PENNY'S WORTH OF CHARACTER
THE BEATINEST BOY

Library of Congress Catalog Card Number: 55-11574

Published by Whittlesey House
A division of the McGraw-Hill Book Company, Inc.
Printed in the United States of America

To
JESSE LEE RAMEY

CONTENTS

Red Mule Has a Helper   13

Scrappie's Mother Has a Guest   24

Red Mule Sees a Way Out   34

Scrappie Talks with His Father   48

Scrappie Goes Home with the Mules   60

The Big Surprise   68

Scrappie's Father Makes a Decision   79

Mules Triumph over Tractors   92

Scrappie Finds a Way   109

RED MULE

Red Mule Has a Helper

Red Mule stood under the leafy elm and watched Scrappie as he drove the span of big mules hitched to a disk harrow across the lot to the shade. The mules were getting wet with perspiration and Scrappie knew how much the mules could stand. He had been working mules for almost two years now. When Scrappie drove them toward the elm, Red Mule waited for him with a smile on his face.

13

"Scrappie, you're going to make a great teamster," he said. "You like mules. And when you like them, they like you. I've liked mules since I was so small I had to stand up in the barn mangers to fasten the collars around their necks. You're just like I was when I was twelve years old. You're the only boy left around here who likes mules."

"Gee, Red Mule, I'm proud of what you've said to me," Scrappie told him.

Scrappie sat on the springy seat of the disk harrow with the leather check lines in his hand. His face was tanned by the spring wind and sun. He didn't wear a hat and his black hair was tousled by the wind.

"You taught me to like mules," he said.

Scrappie smiled as he watched Red Mule put his big hand on Dick's back to wipe off the loose hair he was shedding for spring.

Just then Milford Royster drove his tractor into the four lots across the street. When Red Mule saw him driving in he stopped rubbing loose hairs from Dick's back. He watched Milford

14

set his plows down and start his tractor around
the lots. The two plows were turning the
dark dirt over fast. The tractor engine sang a
song Red Mule and Scrappie didn't like to hear.
Red Mule plugged his ears with his big index
fingers. Scrappie looked toward the tractor
and the smile left his face. Even Dick and
Dinah didn't like to hear the song that the tractor
sang.

"Do you reckon old Milford likes his tractor
as much as we like our mules?" Red Mule
shouted.

"I don't see how he could," Scrappie replied
as loud as he could holler. "The tractor can't
put its mouth on his shoulder and nibble when it
wants something. The tractor can't talk to
him."

"So you've learned mules can talk," Red
Mule said with a big grin. When he grinned
he showed Scrappie a mouthful of big teeth behind his red beard. "When you're sure they
talk, that's when you fall in love with them and
they fall in love with you." Red Mule spoke

15

softer now, for the tractor was on the other side. "You'll be a real mule man when you grow up. People around here will be calling you Mule too. Only you don't have red hair like I have. They might call you Young Mule. Then they might start calling me Old Mule instead of Red Mule. You'll be Young Mule and I'll be Old Mule. Listen to that awful tractor!"

The tractor had circled back again and its harsh song was louder in Red Mule's and Scrappie's ears. But Dick and Dinah, a fine-looking pair of big mules, stood very quietly on the soft ground. The only time either raised a foot or swished a tail was when he was bitten by a blue-tail fly. Dick and Dinah didn't like flies. Scrappie didn't either. When one of the flies came around, Scrappie got off the harrow and caught it. Red Mule had shown him how to do this. Scrappie would ease up close and then slap his hand over the fly. He'd got so he never missed.

"Red Mule, I believe mules can understand our talk too," Scrappie said. "Old Dick and

16

Dinah are listening right now to what we're saying about them."

"Sure, they're listening," Red Mule agreed. "Mules have a way of listening to what is said about them. And this is the reason many men are kicked by mules. A man has to be awfully mean to say anything bad about a mule. He deserves to be kicked."

"I've worked Dick and Dinah long enough until I believe they can understand me, and I know I can understand them," Scrappie said. "I can't tell this to my father and mother and a lot of other people. They wouldn't believe me." Scrappie had to shout, for Milford was circling back with his tractor. "But now I know they can. And I'd rather hear mules talking any time than hear a tractor's groaning song!"

"When Milford first got that tractor," Red Mule told Scrappie, "I said to myself, 'It's goin' to be hard on me and my mules. There might even come a time when we won't get enough to eat!' I saw right then, Scrappie, hard times were coming, and I've been plowing lots around this town over forty years. I could see it was trouble, Scrappie."

"Do you think we're goin' to lose out?" Scrappie asked, looking up at him.

"I don't know, Scrappie," Red Mule said as he watched Milford fly around the lots on his tractor. "He can plow four lots while we're plowing one. He has hurt our business with that thing. I used to plow all the lots in Blakesburg and now I don't get a fourth of the spring gardens and truck patches to plow. Milford has hurt my business."

"That's all right, Red Mule," Scrappie said. "We'll fight for the business."

"Yes, the tractors are hurting us," Red Mule continued. "But I still think there's a place in the world for mules. I think this country has a great need for mules!"

"Look, he's going to finish plowing and disking four lots before we get one plowed and disked," Scrappie sighed.

"Let 'im go," Red Mule said. "Let 'im do it. You give Dick and Dinah their time. They might be slow compared to that tractor but they get there just the same. Just don't rush mules and try to do as much as Milford's tractor."

"I won't, Red Mule," Scrappie told him. "You've always taught me that if I let the mule stay in his own gait, he'll be very slow to tire."

"You're a lot lighter on that disk than I am," Red Mule said. "I'm too much of a load for the mules to pull on a disk that cuts deep in plowed ground. So you go on, Scrappie."

"Get up, Dick and Dinah," Scrappie called, shaking the lines in his hands. "You've had a good rest now. Let's take another round or two before dinnertime."

Scrappie spoke to them just like Red Mule. He used the same words that Red Mule used. The mules stepped briskly, pulling the heavy disk harrow through the soft ground. Scrappie sat up proudly with the leather check lines in his hands just like he had seen Red Mule sit upon the wagon and drive Dick and Dinah through Blakesburg.

When Red Mule watched Scrappie drive the

mules, he smiled. But when he turned to look across the street at Milford Royster, the smile left his face. "We'd better quit for dinner, Scrappie," Red Mule said.

Scrappie drove the mules over to the elm shade and stopped them. Then Red Mule walked over and unhitched Dinah while Scrappie unhitched Dick from the disk. They unhooked the trace chains and wrapped them around the back bands. Each folded a leather check line up in a bundle and tied it with the end of the line and hung it over a hame above the mule's collar. Red Mule led Dinah, and Scrappie led Dick over to the wagon. Here Red Mule poured feed from a sack into the feedboxes.

"I'll water them before you get back, Scrappie," Red Mule said.

"Where's your dinner, Red Mule?" Scrappie asked, looking into the wagon.

"I didn't bring any today," he replied.

"But won't you get hungry?" Scrappie asked.

Red Mule looked at Scrappie and grinned. "Oh, sometimes I do," he said. "But shucks, I

20

ain't done much work this morning. You, Dick, and Dinah have done the work. I've just stood around and watched you and Milford and his tractor."

"But you'll get hungry, Red Mule," Scrappie said. "Come home with me and eat."

Scrappie invited Red Mule before he thought. Suddenly he hoped Red Mule wouldn't accept his invitation, because he had heard his mother talk so much about Red Mule's being dirty. He'd heard his mother's friends say, too, they had to stop breathing when they passed Red Mule on the street because he smelled. But Scrappie knew better, and he had tried to explain to his mother that the smell on Red Mule wasn't caused by dirt. He knew what kind of smell it was. It was mule smell.

Red Mule stood there looking at Scrappie, trying to make up his mind whether to go or not. Then he said, "I'd better not go today. Thank you, Scrappie!"

When Scrappie had walked a few steps, he turned to look back. Red Mule didn't see him, but he saw Red Mule dip his hand into the feed-

box and come up with a handful of horse-and-mule feed.

Scrappie watched Red Mule take a big bite of the feed from his hand, then brush the feed from his whiskers. He knew Red Mule was hungry. Scrappie was hungry too, but as he walked toward his home his hunger went away.

Scrappie's Mother Has a Guest

"Wash your hands and face now, Scrappie," his mother called just as he walked upon the porch. "You're late."

"Mom, I'll wash my face and hands but I'm not hungry," he said.

His pretty mother, Mary Lykins, looked very strangely at her son. She thought he might be sick. He always came home hungry when he worked with Red Mule. He came home and he and his mother always ate together. His father ate at The Dinner Bell, which was down the street from his grocery store. His father could take only a few minutes for his lunch.

"What's the matter with you, Scrappie?" his mother asked him. "Are you sick?"

"No, Mom, I'm not sick," he replied.

"Did something go wrong?" she asked him.

"Mom, poor old Red Mule hasn't any lunch."

"Well, he could have, couldn't he?" she said, looking at Scrappie with her soft blue eyes. "He gets paid for every garden he plows, doesn't he? And he's never paid you anything for helping him. He's promised you, I know, but has he ever paid you?"

"He's got his mules to feed, Mom," Scrappie replied. "He doesn't get as many gardens to plow as he used to. Milford Royster gets them to plow with his tractor. Jed Warnock and Sylvester Lybrooks have got tractors too and they're getting gardens around here to plow. Everybody who gets a tractor hurts Red Mule. He's had a hard winter because he didn't get much work to do. I don't care whether he pays me or not."

His mother didn't frown but Scrappie thought she was going to. She wasn't a bit pleased with what Scrappie had said.

"Come on now and eat your lunch," she told him. "It's going to get cold."

"Mom, I can't eat when I know Red Mule is hungry," he said.

"How do you know he's hungry?" she asked.

"I saw him take a handful of feed from Dick's box when I looked back," he said with tears welling up in his eyes. "A man has to be hungry to eat horse-and-mule feed."

"But he's so. . . ."

"He's not that dirty, Mom," Scrappie interrupted. "I work with Red Mule and I know. I know he smells like a hot mule and he walks like a tired one. But I like mule smell."

"Maybe I've got enough cooked for both of you," she told Scrappie. "Go tell him to come over and eat with you."

Scrappie jumped up from the table. He wiped the tears from his eyes with the back of his hand. He was smiling when he ran out the door. He didn't take time to go down one step at a time. He jumped all the way and took off running down the street. He ran until he reached Red Mule, standing beside the wagon watching Dick and Dinah.

"Red Mule, I've got good news!" Scrappie cried. "Mom wants you to come over to our house and eat with me today."

"That's wonderful, Scrappie," Red Mule said. "But I ain't hungry."

"I know you are, too, Red Mule," Scrappie said. "Now, come on. If you don't, I'll stop working for you."

"Then I'll go along," he told Scrappie. "I don't want you to stop working for me, because you like mules. You'll make the greatest mule man around here one of these days."

Big Red Mule and little Scrappie walked

27

away together while Dick and Dinah ate contentedly from the feedboxes in the wagon.

Red Mule took his big black umbrella hat off just as he climbed up onto the porch. Scrappie started through the door and Red Mule was following.

"Ouch," Red Mule groaned.

"What's the matter, Red Mule?" Scrappie asked as he turned around to see.

"I bumped my head," he said. "Shucks, that's not anything unusual."

"How tall are you, Red Mule?" Scrappie asked.

"I don't know exactly," he answered. "I haven't measured in a long time. But I 'spect I'm about six feet four, maybe six feet six."

"Bend over and watch the doors," Scrappie warned him. "Don't bump again. The door into the breakfast nook might be lower than this one."

Red Mule followed Scrappie through the living room, where he walked slowly and looked at the nice furniture, the starched, white, ruffled window curtains, and the flowered rug beneath his feet. This house was very strange to him. He'd never been in a home this nice since his mother had died, many years ago. Red Mule stooped for another door. He followed Scrappie into the dining room, where his head touched the chandelier and the little glass beads rattled. Red Mule looked at the wallpaper, the chest, the big cupboard, and the long table in this room. On the wall was a picture of fruit that made him really hungry.

"Watch this door, Red Mule," Scrappie said.

Red Mule stooped and then he turned his shoulders sideways so he could get through.

"Gee, Red Mule, I didn't know you were so big!" Scrappie exclaimed. "No wonder you don't ride the disk. I'll bet you live in a house with high doors."

"Well, I guess you would call the doors to my house pretty high," he laughed.

"Red Mule, you've never met Mom," Scrappie said. "This is my mother."

"I'm Mary Lykins," she said, looking up at big Red Mule.

Scrappie looked at his small, pretty mother

with dainty hands. When Red Mule reached his big hand to shake hers, she reached hers gently, and when Red Mule had shaken her hand, she jerked it back as if she were afraid.

"Mrs. Lykins, I've seen you before but I didn't know you were Scrappie's mother," Red Mule said as he looked down at the small table filled with food. "I know your husband, Frank, very well."

"Scrappie and I always eat our lunch in this breakfast nook," she said. "I hope you'll find room enough to be comfortable."

"Oh, I'll be all right, Mrs. Lykins," Red Mule said. His head was just under the ceiling. "There's plenty of room in here."

The little table was filled with food. Scrappie sat down on one side and Red Mule on the other.

"Of course I've not fixed anything extra, since I didn't know any one was coming," Mrs. Lykins said. "But I hope there'll be enough of what we have."

"You have plenty here for us, Mrs. Lykins," Red Mule said as he squeezed between the table and the wall. "Scrappie wanted me to come home and eat with 'im. Scrappie's goin' to make a wonderful mule man. The mules like him, and he likes the mules."

"Yes, I know a lot about Dick and Dinah," she said. "Now, Scrappie, you and Red Mule can help yourselves to the food. I'll leave you alone. You will excuse me."

Scrappie was really hungry now and he started reaching and helping himself. Red Mule's long arms could reach across the little table and beyond. He towered over the table like old Dick or Dinah would have, if they had been sitting in chairs and eating from this table. He had to spread his legs out under the table right past Scrappie's chair. And if he'd pulled them up, his knees would have lifted the little table.

Red Mule was helping himself to the ham and eggs. He put four of the eight fried eggs on his plate. Then he helped himself to a good helping of ham.

"Mom put some extras on the table while I went back to get you," Scrappie told Red Mule.

"I guess she thought that she didn't have enough for a couple of mule drivers like us."

"That's it, Scrappie," Red Mule said as he put the loaded fork through his beard to his mouth.

Only once the door opened and Mrs. Lykins came in. "Are you getting along all right?" she asked. "Is there enough for two hungry men?"

"Plenty, ma'am," Red Mule answered.

"Are you getting along all right, Scrappie?"

"Yes, Mom," he replied. "We're hungry and this is a wonderful lunch."

"If you need me, Scrappie, call me," she told him.

"All right, Mom," he said. "But Red Mule and I are getting along fine."

She turned and left the breakfast nook.

"It's a wonderful meal," Red Mule said as he got up from the table and looked at the white, ruffled tieback curtains. Red Mule stood and looked at them as if they were something not to touch. "I guess we'd better be getting back to Dick and Dinah," he said. "They've had a good rest."

33

Red Mule Sees a Way Out

"Scrappie, you lead Dick to the water hole and I'll take Dinah," Red Mule said. "You know where we have to take them to water."

"It's funny about mules," Scrappie remarked. "Can you tell me why it is they wade up and down a creek and smell the water? Then they find a place where they want to drink. If Dick and Dinah can't get back to this hole, they won't drink any place in Town Branch. They'll do without water until they get home."

"Scrappie, that's what I've always told you," Red Mule spoke softly as they led the big mules behind them down a little-used, unpaved street in Blakesburg. "Mules are smart. Now if you had to drink from Town Branch and could select the place, wouldn't you choose the place Dick and Dinah did? It's a nice, clean hole of deep blue water and it's under the shade of big overhanging willows that keep it cool."

"I never thought about it that way, Red Mule, but you're right," Scrappie said. "Dick and Dinah are smart."

The big man and the small boy led the mules down to Town Branch. Here the street turned into a country road. It crossed the stream. There wasn't any bridge here. And a cloud of early-spring butterflies rose up from the sand. The butterflies were so thick Scrappie and Red Mule had to wait for them to scatter on the wind. The butterflies rose up like a fluttering cloud of many colors and thinned on the bright April wind. Then Scrappie and Red Mule left the road and led the mules up the stream toward the grove of willows, whose leafy tops were green clouds resting on the wind.

Scrappie looked upstream at the deep hole of

35

clean, blue water. The mules took longer steps, getting close to Red Mule's and Scrappie's heels. But they stepped faster and let the mules get to the water. The mules waded into the deep hole to their knees while Scrappie and Red Mule held the bridle reins and watched them put their mouths down into the water and start drinking. They made a little noise as they quenched their thirst after eating the dry horse-and-mule feed.

After they had taken Dick and Dinah back and hitched them to the disk harrow, Scrappie climbed upon the seat.

"We'll get it finished this afternoon," Red Mule said. "I can't collect until the lots have been plowed, harrowed, and the rows laid off."

"Get up, Dick and Dinah," Scrappie said bravely. He was so small sitting upon the disk-harrow seat, with power at his finger tips in the check lines. "Dick and Dinah, we'll take our time but we must have it ready this afternoon so Red Mule can collect."

The mules stepped along in their slow pace. They moved the heavy disk harrow, which ground the big clods almost as fine as sand. Before the afternoon was half over, Red Mule scooped up a big handful of the dark dirt and let it sift through his fingers. He grinned as he brushed the last grains of dirt from his big hands. Then he walked across the street to see what kind of plowing and disking Milford Royster had done for Ike Abrahams.

He walked around the edge of the ground Milford had plowed. Then he walked out into the plowed earth. "Scrappie," he called.

"Yes, Red Mule," Scrappie answered as he reined his mules to a stop.

"Come over here a minute," Red Mule shouted. "I want to show you something."

Scrappie drove Dick and Dinah back to the maple shade and fastened the check lines onto the seat. Then, he ran across the road to where Red Mule was standing in the middle of the land Milford had plowed and harrowed.

"Reckon they won't get us for trespassing?" Scrappie said. "We'll tramp that plowed ground by walking over it."

"We can't hurt this ground." Red Mule told him. "Come on!"

Red Mule had the biggest grin on his face Scrappie had ever seen. He was showing all of his teeth now. And the long red hair on his head blew out behind him like a long red streamer when he took his umbrella hat off. The April wind pressed the long red beard down against his face for he faced the April wind.

"Look, Scrappie," Red Mule said in a loud voice and then he laughed louder than the blowing wind. "Come, look at this dirt! See how Milford leaves it! Does this look like soft garden dirt where Ike can plant his peas, corn, and potatoes? How can Ike ever make a lettuce bed in this kind of dirt? How can he sow radish, carrot, and beet seeds in ground like this?"

Scrappie looked at the coarse lumps of dirt in Red Mule's hand. There were three clods as big as lumps of coal.

"Looks like that ground was plowed wet once," Scrappie said.

"Plowed wet, my red whiskers," Red Mule shouted. "Old Milford was in too big a hurry to get to the next lot. He missed these clods with his disk! We might get this job to do over!

See Milford is in a big hurry to get all the lots and to squeeze me and the mules out! He wants all the trade. He wants to starve us out. He's made his brags he'd send me, old Red Mule, to the poorhouse!"

"This ground is not half plowed," Scrappie said as he stooped down and tried to lift a big clod. "How can Milford Royster do this to people? How can he get by?"

"Scrappie, we wouldn't get a lot to plow if we did a job like this," Red Mule said. "You know we wouldn't! Look all the way around beside this fence, Scrappie! Look, there's a four-foot strip that's not plowed at all. Maybe Milford was afraid of getting his tractor scratched on the fence. We wouldn't leave that much ground! That's why we bring the little plow and use one mule when we plow up close to the fence. I was sad up until now, for I thought Milford was going to send me to the poorhouse. Now I know he's not."

Red Mule threw the big clods up over the top of a maple and they came down and hit more clods and still didn't break. And then Red

Mule laughed louder than any wind Scrappie had ever heard blowing up this street since winter. He laughed louder than Dick and Dinah ever brayed! He picked up more clods and threw them into the leaves on the trees.

"What's the matter over there?" Scrappie knew the voice. He turned to look as Red Mule heaved the big clods up into the leafy elm.

"Is old Red Mule having some sort of fit?" Mrs. Ezra Williams had stopped just across the street. She was a close friend of Scrappie's mother. She will go straight home and tell Mom, Scrappie thought quickly. She's one of the women in the town who walks on the far side of the street when she meets Red Mule.

"Oh, no, Mrs. Williams, Red Mule is all right," Scrappie replied. "There's not anything wrong with Red Mule! He's all right. He's throwing at a lizard, snake, bird, or something up there in that tree!"

"I don't see anything up there for him to throw at," she said. "If you were my son, I'd be more particular about whom you loaf with. I don't understand your mother sometimes!"

41

Mrs. Williams walked on down the street toward Scrappie's home in a hurry. Red Mule heaved more big clods up into the trees. Red Mule was rejoicing and Scrappie rejoiced with him. Scrappie picked up smaller clods and threw them up and laughed too.

That afternoon Scrappie finished harrowing the ground. Then Red Mule hitched Dinah to the little single-shovel plow he used for laying off the rows. Scrappie set stakes at each end of the lot while Red Mule reined Dinah toward the stakes. When he had finished, the rows were straight as ramrods. Then Red Mule and Scrappie lifted the single-shovel plow and the big turning plow up into the wagon and chained the disk behind.

"Now hitch the team onto the wagon while I go collect," Red mule said.

Red Mule went across the street to Fain Meadows' home and when he returned, there was a big smile on his face again. Scrappie knew he had his pay. Scrappie was sitting upon the seat, with the mules ready to go. Dick and

Dinah were prancing as if they hadn't worked at all and were not tired. They knew this was the end of the day and they were going home.

"Are you ready, Red Mule?" Scrappie said.

"I'm ready," he said. "The job is done. I had to wait, but I've got some money now to buy feed for my mules and food for myself."

"All right, Dick and Dinah," Scrappie said. "Let's go. Red Mule is ready."

The mules walked faster than their usual pace. They pulled the wagon onto the street and there was an awful noise as the disk clattered behind. Scrappie sat up on the springy seat, holding the lines. Scrappie looked over hard at the truck drivers who drove close to the team. If one got behind the wagon and blew his horn, Red Mule looked back then and the truck driver didn't blow his horn any more.

"You know, Scrappie, I heard the mayor was going to stop me from chaining my disk harrow on behind the wagon and going down the street," Red Mule shouted in Scrappie's ear. "He said my disk made too much noise."

"Who do you think reported us, Red Mule?"

"Oh, it's hard to tell," Red Mule hollered. "Mayor Stewart says there's a town ordinance against disk harrows on the street. This town has changed since I was a boy. I used to ride up and down these streets on my disk with a red-handled whip over my shoulder. I carried a whip for decoration but never used it. I had red tassels on my mules' bridles. But this was before 1922, when they paved the streets in this town. I was seventeen then. It was a good ride back in them days on the old disk harrow behind Rock and Ruth!"

Many cars pulled up behind the wagon and couldn't go around for the oncoming traffic. It was quitting time in Blakesburg for shop-keepers and men who worked in the town. They were driving to their homes in the town and in the country. When the long line formed behind the mules and wagon, many of the drivers started blowing their horns. Red Mule looked back, but Scrappie couldn't look now. He had to look ahead and watch the traffic. Dick and Dinah didn't like to walk on the streets in the first place. They liked to step on earth, where

there was a little soft spring beneath their steel shoes. And they didn't like to have trucks and automobiles get too close to them. The disk was making a great noise on the concrete.

"Red Mule, I'll scoot over and let you have the mules now," Scrappie said. "I'll soon be getting out."

"Won't you go home with me, Scrappie?" Red Mule asked him.

This was the first time Red Mule had ever asked Scrappie to go home with him.

"Gee, Red Mule, I'd like to go home with you and Dick and Dinah," Scrappie said. "But I can't this afternoon. I'll have to ask Mom and Dad."

"Can you go home with me tomorrow night?" Red Mule asked as he slid over and took the lines from Scrappie.

"I'll ask them tonight and I'll let you know in the morning," Scrappie replied.

Red Mule drove up and stopped right in front of Scrappie's home so he could get off the wagon. At the same time, Scrappie's father drove up the street and turned left in front of the mules, who were holding up a long line of honking cars now. He drove into his driveway and stopped. He looked from the window of his car at the line of traffic, which looked like a funeral procession. And then he heard the great noise of the disk following the wagon as Red Mule drove on down the street and Scrappie came running across the yard.

"Scrappie, Scrappie," Red Mule called back as he reined his mules to a stop. "I forgot to tell you. We'll plow the potato patch for Dave Bishop in the morning and you know. . . ."

But the honking of the cars drowned out Red Mule's words. He and his mules had to move on while Scrappie and his father stood looking at the long line of creeping automobiles behind the team and wagon. Big Red Mule was sitting up on the springboard seat, brave as a lion. He held the check lines in his hand.

"Well, if that's not a picture of progress, Scrappie," Frank Lykins said to his son. "Look at that, won't you! Look at the automobiles that old plug team is holding back!"

"Dad, Dick and Dinah are not a plug mule team," Scrappie told his father. "Do you know what a plug team is? Dad, a plug team is one that's so old it can hardly walk, let alone pull a load. I've been driving Dick and Dinah today. They're young and powerful!"

"They don't look like it the way they're going up that street, holding up half the traffic in this town," his father said.

"But, Dad, Red Mule has to come this way to get out of town," Scrappie explained. "This is the only way he can go to the Sandee River bridge. Any other street would take him out of town on a different road. He has to cross the Sandee River to get home. Red Mule doesn't want to hold up traffic. He doesn't like traffic. He wants it to get past him and his mules."

"Then in this modern age he shouldn't be driving a team of slow mules," Frank Lykins told his son. "Our modern highways are made for automobiles and not mules. In this mechanical age we have to have speed, for we have so many people. Mules are too slow and out of place on our modern highways!"

"Dad, mules have a gait and that's the way to let them walk," Scrappie explained. "Red Mule never lets his mules get out of their gait and they can work all day long."

"I'm glad to know that, Scrappie," Frank Lykins said, laying his hand on his son's tousled head. "I'll admit I know more about the grocery business than I do about mules. I've

49

never ridden on the back of a mule, nor have I driven a team of mules in my life."

"You've missed a lot, Dad," Scrappie said, looking up and smiling at his father.

"Come along, Son, let's go in the house," his father requested. "I want to talk with you."

Scrappie followed his father up the steps and into the living room. Then Frank Lykins pulled off his shoes and put his feet into his soft slippers.

"When you grow up and get older, Scrappie, you'll have to learn how wonderful it is to relax," his father said.

Scrappie watched him sit down in his big soft chair and put his feet up on a stool. His mother had left the Auckland *Daily News* on the arm of his chair. "Yes, I come home from the store and I'm ready to drop," he talked on as he pulled a cigar from his inside coat pocket, lit it with a lighter, and puffed a cloud of smoke. "And I like to be with you and Mother. I like to sit here in my good soft chair and smoke and take it easy until supper is ready."

"Frank, you can't guess who we had for

lunch today." It was Scrappie's mother. She came from the kitchen, smiling. "I'll give you ten guesses."

"It couldn't have been Red Mule?"

"You guessed it, Dad," Scrappie said.

"Oh, no!" he said. "I was just teasing when I guessed he'd had lunch with you. How could he ever get vittles inside his mouth with all that beard he's got? His face looks like a crow's nest made of red sticks."

"Red Mule is a fine man," Scrappie said. "But he's hungry. I saw 'im eating feed from the mules' feedbox. I came on home for my lunch but I couldn't eat for thinking about him. So Mom let me go back and bring him home to eat with me."

"Well, I hope this doesn't become a habit," his father said. "How do you feel about it, Mother? Do you want to cook for Red Mule?"

"Well, I can't say that I do, Frank," she replied. "He will eat as much as a family of four. . . ."

"But Red Mule is hungry, Mom," Scrappie interrupted her.

52

"Lucy came by and told me she saw Red Mule throwing at something up in a tree and said she never heard such laughing as he was doing," Scrappie's mother said. "Lucy said after she walked down the street and looked back you were throwing too."

"Mom, I saw Mrs. Williams on the other side of the street," Scrappie explained. "I knew how she'd talked about Red Mule. And she stopped there to find out something to run and tell you. She asked me what was the matter with Red Mule, why he was doing all that laughing."

"Tell us, Son, what did tickle Red Mule?" his father said.

Scrappie told his father how Red Mule had found big clods of earth in the lot Milford had plowed. "Red Mule knew then, Dad," Scrappie went on, "that the tractors weren't going to put his mules out of business and he was so happy he yelled and laughed. And he threw some of the dirt up into the tree."

"Well, people are also talking about the way you work for Red Mule and never get paid,

Scrappie," his father said. "When is Red Mule going to pay you?"

"Dad, Red Mule needs his money," Scrappie said. "He's got to eat. He's got to feed Dick and Dinah!"

"Are you going to be another Red Mule?" Frank Lykins asked, looking seriously at his son. "Now a lot of people have asked me. Everybody in this town knows how you tag around after Red Mule. They know how you sit up there and drive mules through town hitched to a wagon loaded with plows, hoes, and feed-boxes, with a disk harrow chained on behind. People laugh when they see you coming with a long string of cars honking behind you. Son, that's a picture of progress!"

"But, Dad, I like Dick and Dinah and the wagon better than a car," Scrappie admitted.

"Well, you probably won't when you're a year or two older. Now let me tell you something, Son, about Red Mule," Frank Lykins spoke in a serious tone. "I remember the time when he was a respectable young man in this town. I was about your age then."

"Dad, isn't Red Mule still a respectable man in this town?" Scrappie exclaimed. "What is the matter with Red Mule?"

"Oh, yes, he's a law-abiding man and good in many ways," Scrappie's father started explaining, "but he's gone to seed. You know what we mean when we say something has gone to seed?"

"Not exactly," Scrappie replied.

"When something goes to seed, it's all through," his father continued to explain. "It hasn't any more value. That's the way people around here look at Red Mule. And mules are through too. They're things of the past. They have no more usefulness. Old lazy mules have been Red Mule's downfall. I'll bet you don't even know his real name."

"Red Mule is his name to me," Scrappie said.

"That's the name all this young generation know him by," Frank Lykins said. "But his real name is Gabriel Gullet. That's a prettier name than Red Mule, isn't it?"

"Not to me," Scrappie said. "That doesn't even sound like it ought to be his name. Red Mule is more like it."

"Scrappie, there was a time when Red Mule plowed gardens in this town and made money," his father explained. "He lived in that little red-brick house on the river front where Donald Dunnaway lives now. He had a livery stable back on Second Street near the Mendall Blacksmith Shop. Gabriel Gullet lived with his mother. His father, Cy Gullet, died when Gabriel was younger than you are now. Gabriel made money in those days. He wore fine clothes and he drove the best-looking horses, with red tassels on their bridles, brass knobs on their hames, and little bells that jingled on their polished harnesses. Since the horse-and-buggy days, we've had the automobile and the air age and now we're in the mechanical age. Old Gabriel is still living in the horse-and-buggy days. He's fooled around with mules too long. Now, do you want to grow up and be a man like him?"

"Yes, Dad, I'd like to be like Red Mule," Scrappie admitted quietly. "I don't think I want to work in a grocery store, Dad."

"There's plenty of ways to make a living

besides driving mules or running a grocery either," his father said. "You'll probably have a dozen ideas before you decide. Red Mule lives somewhere out of Blakesburg, doesn't he? No one seems to know exactly where he does live."

"Dad, he's asked me to go home with him tomorrow night," Scrappie said. "That's what I want to ask you."

Frank Lykins looked at his son.

"Yes," he said slowly, "you can go. I want you to find out whether you really want to be a mule driver!"

"Frank, do you think that's all right?" Scrappie's mother asked as she came from the kitchen, where she was preparing supper. "Are you sure of what you are doing?"

"Oh, yes, Mother," he said, "I'm quite sure. One of these days Scrappie will be a big boy and he'll be wearing a nice suit of clothes and have a pretty girl holding onto his arm. There won't be any more Red Mule and mule teams then. Let him go now and enjoy himself! Let 'im be a real boy!"

"Gee, Dad, that's wonderful!" Scrappie shouted as he jumped up from his chair and put his arm around his father's neck. "You've made me very happy!"

"But, Frank," Mary Lykins argued, "where does Red Mule live? Do you know, Scrappie?"

"No, I don't, Mom," he replied. "But if you'll let me go, I'll tell you after tomorrow night."

"But, Scrappie, I'll worry about you," she said. "I'll be wondering about what kind of a bed you'll be sleeping in and what you'll have to eat. I just can't imagine Red Mule's cooking anything you can eat."

"Now, Mother, quit worrying and let Scrappie and me handle this," Frank Lykins said with a wink. "Red Mule's like a boy when it comes to animals. Let Scrappie go with him. Let Scrappie worry about something to eat and a bed to sleep in. He won't starve overnight without your cooking."

"Dad, I'll always love you for this," Scrappie said as he took his arm from his father's neck. "I'll never be able to go to sleep tonight for thinking about going home with Red Mule tomorrow night."

Frank Lykins chuckled and rumpled Scrappie's hair. "It will be a real experience for you, Son. I'll be interested to hear all about your visit when you get home."

Scrappie Goes Home with the Mules

"It's hard to believe I'm going home with you," Scrappie said as they finished work the next day.

"I've wanted to explain something to you for quite a while, Scrappie," Red Mule said, looking straight ahead and down the street. "You must have thought it strange that I've been sharing the work with you but not the money for the work."

"That's all right, Red Mule. I don't care about money."

"It's not reasonable that you shouldn't, but

I think you'll understand after you visit with me tonight. I've had something in my mind for a long time. You're in for a big surprise tonight, Scrappie!"

"Gee, that's wonderful talk, Red Mule." Scrappie was excited. "I can hardly wait to know what it is. I know it will be good. I've always known, Red Mule, that you are fair and honest about anything you do. I've never worried about your not paying me. I've enjoyed working with you."

They continued down Main Street and the cars whizzed past them.

"Hiya, Red Mule," Bouncer Gilliam yelled from the sidewalk as they passed. "Hiya, Little Mule!"

Then Bouncer ran away, laughing. Scrappie watched Bouncer from the corner of his eye as he ran around behind the courthouse. He laughed and pointed to Scrappie and Red Mule.

"I'll make him laugh one of these days," Scrappie told Red Mule. "He's been getting smart with me because I work with you."

"Pay no attention to him," Red Mule said.

"There's a lot of people like him. They don't have any fun in life and don't want anybody else to have fun."

"I know Bouncer," Scrappie said. "I have to go to school with him. He pokes fun at you and me."

"Now, Scrappie, never worry about that." Red Mule spoke softly. "There are bigger things in this world to worry about. The surprise I'm going to show you tonight is one."

When they left Blakesburg they drove across a bridge over the Sandee River. It was a narrow bridge, built seventy-five years ago in the horse-and-buggy days. Cars had to wait on each end now when a team went over. The teams that crossed in one day could be counted on the fingers on one hand and there would be fingers left, but when a team went over, it took a few minutes and the cars would be lined up on each end waiting. But Red Mule, Scrappie, Dick, and Dinah had to cross the river and the cars had to wait.

When they reached U.S. 23, the cars zoomed past them like big bullets on singing wheels.

"Scrappie, I remember when this was a plain old dirt road," Red Mule sighed wistfully. "It was a pretty road with a lot of curves. The dirt was soft on the mules' feet. I've come over this road many times before with my wagon loaded in April. Those old apple trees up there are about all that's natural here. They're white with blooms again this year. They've been white with blossoms every year since I can remember. I remember another world here, Scrappie, a wonderful world of powerful mule and horse teams, rubber-tired buggies, fringed surreys, express wagons, and jolt wagons. I wish you could have known that world, Scrappie!"

"I wish I could have too," Scrappie said.

But mules do hold up traffic, Scrappie thought. They are slow, like Dad said. This is a faster age. Scrappie was thinking of the Sandee River bridge they had just crossed and how they held up traffic. He didn't tell Red Mule his thoughts.

They reached Colton's Branch and turned to their left.

"See, we've even got a hard road up this creek," Red Mule exclaimed. "Got it four years ago. Not many soft dirt roads left for the mules and horses. But we'll soon be on one."

"Get up, Dick and Dinah," Scrappie said happily.

"Turn right here and we'll get on a good mule road."

Scrappie reined Dick and Dinah onto a narrow road between two high hills.

"Watch 'em step on this soft road, won't you?" Red Mule shouted above the noise of the creaking wagon. "They like it."

Scrappie looked up to his right, then over to his left at the high, wonderful hills, where the trees were beginning to leaf. And alongside this winding little dirt road was a stream that murmured over the rocks as it ran toward the river and the sea.

"Gee, this is pretty country, Red Mule," Scrappie said softly. "I wish we lived out here. How come you ever chose such wonderful country?"

"You know I used to live in Blakesburg, but

it got so that with all this modern living after the cars came, mules and barns were no longer welcome in Blakesburg. So I went with 'em, Scrappie," he replied. "I bought land here and moved to the right fork of Colton's Branch."

They drove up the little road and the farther they went up this valley, the faster Dick and Dinah went.

"First time I ever saw 'em get out of their gait, Red Mule," Scrappie said.

"They're getting close to home," he said. "A mule likes his home. He likes a certain hole of water to drink from, a certain manger and box to eat from, and a certain place to sleep."

Then they reached another place, where two little streams came from two valleys to make the stream and valley they had followed.

"Turn right, Scrappie," Red Mule told him.

The road was very narrow now and the hills were much higher. In a few minutes Scrappie looked up and saw a big barn that looked like it was ready to fall. The road he was following led him into the barn entry. Here the mules stopped.

The Big Surprise

"Well, here's the place," Red Mule said.

"But where's the house, Red Mule?"

"Up there in the hay," he said. "Dick and Dinah and my other mules have their stalls down here."

"Gee, this is wonderful." Scrappie was excited. "I'd like this kind of life."

Scrappie wondered how Red Mule cooked up there in the hay, but he didn't ask him.

They unhitched Dick and Dinah and took the harness from them. Red Mule turned them loose in the lot so they could wallow in the dry dust and then get water from the stream that flowed across the barn lot. Then Red Mule put feed into their boxes and showed Scrappie how to throw hay down from the hayloft into their mangers below. Red Mule had him fork more hay down into the long manger, where there weren't any mule stalls.

"What's all this hay for?" Scrappie shouted down at Red Mule.

"You just wait and see," he hollered back.

As Scrappie came down the ladder from the hayloft, he watched Red Mule walk through the barn entry and to the upper end of the barn lot, where he opened a big, swinging gate. He began calling: "Cope, boys! Cope, girls! Cope, boys! Come on, girls! Come on, boys!"

Suddenly, Scrappie heard the pounding of hoofs! The sound was like thunder in the distance. Then the sound of thunder got closer and Scrappie's heart started beating faster. He started running to a far corner in the barn lot. When he looked up the hollow he saw the mules coming—dozens of mules. When he saw this herd of lively, galloping mules with their heads thrust forward, their ears laid back, and their tails riding on the wind, Scrappie ran for the fence. He climbed up on the fence and started counting. But he lost all count when some of the mules jumped in front of others. His heart was really pounding now. He'd never seen anything as pretty in his lifetime as this herd of young, high-spirited mules. They galloped into the big stall, which took up nearly all of the barn.

"What do you think of 'em?" Red Mule asked as he came walking down after the last mule had leaped through the big barn door.

"I didn't know you had any more mules." Scrappie spoke with excitement. "They're the prettiest things I've ever seen!"

"I've got thirty-five mules here, and old Dick and Dinah make thirty-seven," he told Scrappie.

"But we can't work all these mules," Scrappie said. "What are you going to do with 'em?"

"I'm goin' to save 'em," Red Mule replied.

"Save 'em from what?" Scrappie asked Red Mule.

Red Mule didn't answer him. He started climbing up the ladder again to the hayloft.

"Scrappie, how would you like to own a mule?" Red Mule said as he stopped on the ladder and looked down at Scrappie, who was coming up behind him. "Do you think you'd like to own one?"

"Sure I would," he replied quickly. "If I owned as many mules as you I'd feel like I was the richest man in the world."

"Well," Red Mule said as he started on up, "let's eat our supper and then we'll do some talking."

In one corner of the barn loft, with hay all around them, Red Mule unlocked a big tin box and got out a box of crackers, a block of brown cheese, and a box of brown sugar.

"This is our supper," he told Scrappie. "Now in the morning, we won't have breakfast here. I'll have a cup of coffee at The Dinner Bell. And I'll let you go home for your breakfast."

"That will be all right, Red Mule," Scrappie said as he hungrily eyed the cheese, crackers, and brown sugar.

Red Mule sliced the cheese with his pocketknife and they ate crackers and cheese and brown sugar on crackers. Scrappie had never had a meal like this before. And he had never eaten food that tasted better. He ate heartily as Red Mule gave him food first, then helped himself.

"See, I'm older, Scrappie, than your father," Red Mule told him. "I lived with my mother until she died many years ago and I've lived with my mules ever since."

"Gee, I'd like this kind of life," Scrappie said. "How come you ever found such a good way to live?"

"Scrappie, I found it by circumstance," Red Mule said as he laid a big cracker loaded with brown sugar on his tongue. "Trucks came first

74

and replaced the jolt wagons and teams. We got better roads so the trucks could go faster. Then we got more and bigger trucks. It just about took all the haulin' away from the mule teams and jolt wagons. Still we could use mules for a lot of things. Plowing ground and snaking saw logs from the timber woods. Then we got the tractors with plows and we got tractors even to haul logs from the woods. The mules didn't have any work left for them. Then men started buying 'em up and hauling 'em away to be butchered for fertilizer and dog food. Ever hear of anything like it?"

"I never did," Scrappie said. He was shocked. "But I do see big truckloads of mules and horses going through Blakesburg."

"They're going to the cannery," Red Mule said. "When I see a truckload of 'em, I turn my head and cry. I really cry, Scrappie. No more work for these good mules and they have to die. It breaks my heart, Scrappie."

Tears welled up in Red Mule's big blue eyes. He sliced more cheese for Scrappie and himself.

"Scrappie, I couldn't have saved all the mules

down there if it hadn't been for you," Red Mule told him.

"How have I helped you, Red Mule?" Scrappie asked, looking up at Red Mule, surprised.

"Well, you've worked for me off and on for almost two years and I've not paid you," Red Mule said. "I've taken the money I should have paid to you and bought more mules!"

"Gee, what's wrong with that?" Scrappie asked. "I'm happy about it. I'm glad I'm helping you save these mules. We're saving 'em together, Red Mule! It makes me happy to know that we are!"

"Well, I'm an honest man, Scrappie," Red Mule said in a soft tone. "People don't work for nothing. I know that I don't expect anybody to work for me for nothing. I've had something in mind a long time, Scrappie."

Scrappie stopped eating and looked straight at Red Mule.

"Scrappie, I'll tell you the real big surprise I have for you," Red Mule said as he held a cracker loaded with brown sugar in his hand.

76

"It wasn't the number of mules I showed you a few minutes ago. Scrappie, I need a partner. I want to make you a junior partner to go into the mule business with me. I want to give you a third of everything!"

"Give me a third!" Scrappie shouted. "You don't mean that, Red Mule?"

"Yes, I do too, Scrappie," he replied softly, looking at the small boy on the hay beside him. "I mean just what I said. You and I can save a lot of mules together. What do you think about it?"

"I want to be your junior partner, Red Mule," he replied. "I know we can work together and save the mules. I'll do all I can to help feed them now. Does it cost a lot of money to feed 'em, Red Mule?"

"All I can make and more too," he said. "If I had the money to buy 'em cheap as they are, and enough land to pasture 'em, I'd own a thousand mules. I'd save that many. It ain't the mules' fault that all this has happened, Scrappie! Mules are as good to work now as they ever were. Mules are industrious. They've

77

lost out. Times have changed. This is another age."

"I hate to hear that," Scrappie said.

"In a hundred years from now boys like you
will be askin' what a mule used to look like,"
Red Mule told him. "I used to have money in
the bank. I had nearly enough to keep me the
rest of my life. But I bought this barn, a hundred acres of land, and all these mules. I don't
have enough land now to pasture my mules, and
that's why I have to feed 'em hay."

"I'll be thinking about feedin' 'em," Scrappie said as his eyes grew heavy with sleep.

That night Red Mule and Scrappie slept on
the hay with quilts over them. Scrappie woke
when the rooster crowed for midnight. He
looked up through the cracks in the barn at the
stars in the blue April sky. And down under
him he heard the loud breathing of the mules.
Now and then two mules would quarrel and one
would squeal and bite the other. Once in the
night he heard Red Mule rise up from his bed of
straw and yell, "Cut it out down there!"

78

Scrappie's Father Makes a Decision

Next morning when Red Mule stopped at The Dinner Bell, Scrappie hurried up the street to his home for breakfast.

He brushed the hay from his clothes carefully before he tried to open the door. It was locked. Then he knocked on the door.

"Just a minute!" Scrappie heard his father's voice. "Take it easy. Just a minute!"

Then the door opened and there stood Frank Lykins in his pajamas, robe, and house slippers.

"Oh, so it's you, Scrappie!" he exclaimed happily. "Mother! Oh, Mother, come and look! Scrappie is here. Come and look where he slept last night!"

Frank Lykins stood in the middle of the door-way until Scrappie's mother came.

"Look, darling, at our Scrappie," he said. Then Frank Lykins laughed loudly. "Mother, I told you to let Scrappie go home with Red Mule."

Scrappie's mother joined his father and they stood looking at Scrappie and shaking with laughter.

"Tell me what's so funny and I'll laugh too," Scrappie told them.

"It's the hay in your hair, Scrappie," his mother said, laughing louder. "You've not washed your face or combed your hair."

Scrappie's hand went up to his head. He felt straw in his hair all right.

"I thought I got it all," he said, turning to walk back down the steps.

"Sure, Dad, I slept in the hay," Scrappie admitted. "And I never slept better in my life."

"Come to breakfast, Scrappie, and tell us all about your visit with Red Mule," his mother said.

"I've got something wonderful to tell you," Scrappie said.

His mother went into the kitchen. Scrappie got all the straw from his hair that he could. Then he went inside the house. I wonder if Red Mule washed this morning, Scrappie thought. I wonder if he combed his hair. He might have washed his face and combed his hair when he first got up this morning. He could have washed in the creek that flows through his barn lot. But if he washed his face and combed his long hair and beard, he did it before I got up.

"Sit down, Son, and join us," his father said. "We want to know about your visit."

"Yes, tell us about it, Scrappie," his mother joined in. "Where does he live?"

"Mom, he lives in a big barn that looks like it's ready to fall," Scrappie said. "But once you get there, it's a swell place. Gee, I liked it out there. Mom, something great has happened. Let me tell. . . ."

"Where is Red Mule's place?" his father interrupted him.

"Up Colton's Branch, then up the right fork

of Colton's Branch, and then up the right fork of the right fork," Scrappie told them.

"You remember well, Scrappie," his father said. "I could follow those directions."

"Did you sleep with anything over you?" his mother asked.

"Oh, yes, a quilt," Scrappie said. "Red Mule and I slept above the mules. We slept on the soft hay under quilts."

"It was cool last night for April," his father said. "I had to set the furnace up ten degrees!"

"Red Mule said it was dogwood winter," Scrappie explained. "But Red Mule said dogwood winter would help him. Said the trees leafed more in a dark, cool time and his mules in that hundred-acre pasture needed green leaves to eat!"

"How many mules has he?" his father asked.

"You mean, how many mules have *we?*" Scrappie corrected. "We have thirty-five out there on the pasture and Dick and Dinah, that we work," Scrappie said. "I'm Red Mule's partner. I own a third of thirty-seven mules! Think of it, Mom! Think of it, Dad! I am rich in mules!"

Scrappie's father was silent. He looked across the table quickly at his wife and she looked at him. It was a worried look that came over Frank Lykins's face, like dark clouds that spread over blue skies before a storm.

"You mean, Scrappie, Red Mule gave you an interest in his mules?" his mother asked him. "You mean he just gave you a third interest in all those mules?"

"Not exactly that way, Mom," Scrappie explained as he ate a hot oatmeal breakfast and drank milk. "See, Mom, it's like this. I've worked for Red Mule after school and Saturdays for almost two years. Red Mule's never paid me. Well, Red Mule took some of the money he should have paid me to buy mules. That's how he has been able to save thirty-seven mules. And this was all right with me. I'm glad he did that and saved the mules. I always told you Red Mule was a good man. He's an honest man too. He wanted to pay me so he gave me one-third interest. Think of it!"

"That's just what I'm doing, Scrappie." Frank Lykins spoke seriously. "Do you realize what it takes to feed thirty-seven mules? Did you know that you will be responsible for one-third of the feed it takes to feed these mules? You could give your one-third interest back to Red Mule and come out ahead financially."

"You don't think I did the right thing?" Scrappie held the spoonful of oatmeal before his mouth. "You want me to give my part of the mules back to Red Mule?"

"No, no, Son, I won't say that," his father said. "I'll say this—you are very young to take on responsibility and have to worry about feeding all those mules. You're taking a great chance!"

"But we are feeding the mules," Scrappie said. "We're plowing lots and truck patches and hauling a few things and buying feed for the mules and food for Red Mule."

Scrappie put the oatmeal in his mouth and ate slowly. His eyes started welling up with tears.

"Frank, remember when you started a little grocery store in this town, you took a chance too," Mary Lykins reminded him. "You made a lot of mistakes, too, in your business but you

85

learned by making them.   Yes, Scrappie is taking a chance but I think we ought to be for his taking a chance!   Look what he has, Frank! Scrappie has one-third of thirty-seven mules! Tell me another boy in this town who has worked like Scrappie and who has as much to show for his work."

"Say, Mary, you do have a point," Frank Lykins said, looking up and smiling at his wife. "You have said something very important. Scrappie does have more than any boy in this town.   He's worked with Red Mule on the side and made it.   He's never missed a day of school, either.   He's been an honor pupil for two years. I think we should help Scrappie work out some easier way to feed his mules!"

"Gee, Dad, that makes me feel wonderful," Scrappie said.   Then a big smile came over Scrappie's face as he dried the tears with the back of his hand.

"Son, give me time to do some thinking about it.   Right now I've got to hurry to the store!"

"And I have to hurry too," Scrappie said. "Red Mule and I are going to work for Tobias

Reffitt today.   Red Mule is already there.   And
my partner needs me."

That evening when Scrappie came into the
living room after supper, Frank Lykins was sitting in his easy chair.

"Scrappie, I've been thinking about what you told me this morning and I've got an idea," his father said. "Sit down and I'll tell you my proposition."

Scrappie sat down in a chair opposite his father.

"You know, Son, I've been thinking about you a lot today," he said softly. "You are now in business. You own mules. When you own something you're responsible for its welfare. You are as responsible for feeding those mules as Red Mule is."

"I know I am, Dad," Scrappie said as he watched his father blow a wisp of smoke toward the ceiling. "That's the reason Red Mule and I worked late today. We got more jobs. We got a job to go over a lot Milford Royster had plowed and disked for Wayne Thompson. He didn't plow close enough to the fence. And he left big clods. So we did that lot after we'd plowed and disked Tobias Reffitt's garden. Dad, I know we've got thirty-seven mules to feed!"

"Scrappie, you're going to learn a lot about

property and progress." His father told him. "Now, you never cared much for the grocery store. Well, I started out with my little store after your mother and I were married. I had a time getting along and making it pay at first. Now I own my store building on Main Street. I don't have to rent my store building any longer. I own this home we live in. And I own three farms. But I've had to work for all of this. And it looks like I've managed pretty well, doesn't it?"

"It sure does, Dad," Scrappie replied. "But, Dad, I never had anything against the grocery store. I just like to work with mules better than in a store."

"The grocery store I have built with my own head and hands has done well for us," Frank Lykins said. "It has bought land enough to pasture your thirty-seven mules and more. I could rent that pasture to somebody for seventy-five dollars a month. I'm willing to rent this pasture to you and Red Mule for your mules!"

"Gee, Dad, that's wonderful," Scrappie said. "But how much will you charge us for thirty-

seven mules?   Red Mule and I can't pay you
seventy-five dollars a month."

"It will take some planning," his father said.
"How about you working for me in the store
part of the time?   Say you work for me by the
hour.   I've been thinking about fifty cents an
hour."

"But I've got to be with Red Mule on some
jobs that are coming up," Scrappie said.

"I know, but you won't be working with Red
Mule all the time," his father said.   "School will
soon be out for the summer and you'll have spare
time.   And besides, I have a lot of things shipped
to me regularly by freight and express that you
and Red Mule can haul from the railway station.
I'll quit hiring Milford Royster to haul them by
truck!"

"It's a bargain, Dad," Scrappie shouted with
joy.   "Red Mule and I will haul your freight
and express from the railway station with our
mules and I'll work for you after school."

"Then my pasture is ready for thirty-seven
mules," his father said.   "Your word is good
enough for me.   You and Red Mule can take

them there any time. The grass is ready for them. This will stop a big feed bill."

"Gee, how wonderful that is, Dad," Scrappie said. "There's no one like my Dad when it comes to solving a problem."

Mules Triumph over Tractors

Before the apple trees had shed their blossoms in the back yards of the homes in Blakesburg, Red Mule and Scrappie had moved their mules to his father's pasture. Spring vacation was over and Scrappie was back at school.

Each day when school was out, Scrappie carried his books into his father's grocery and started work. Some days he filled orders, getting each item down from the shelf as Miss Tyler, the bookkeeper, called it out to him. "One large can of tomatoes," she would say, "one can of corn, cream style, a five-pound sack of sugar."

Scrappie would put the groceries in a carton and get it ready for the delivery boy. Other days, Scrappie would unpack cases and stack the cans in neat pyramids. He often made deliveries when a customer was in a hurry and couldn't wait for the regular delivery.

There were plenty of things that needed to be done all the time in a grocery store. And Scrappie was surprised to find himself getting interested. Salesmen came in with new gadgets and Scrappie's father would call him over and ask his opinion. Sometimes they would decide to buy and sometimes Mr. Lykins just knew it wasn't the kind of thing his customers would want. Scrappie saw that everyone in town had a great deal of respect for his dad's opinions and would ask his advice on all kinds of things having nothing to do with groceries. "Dad, I bet you answer more questions than the mayor does," Scrappie would say, and his father would laugh.

One Saturday afternoon after a particularly busy time, Mr. Lykins said, "Scrappie, you've put in a long, hard day. Why don't you go along home?"

But Scrappie wasn't ready to go. "I'll wait and help Red Mule with the freight load he's bringing in. Dick and Dinah would be disappointed if I didn't give them apples after hauling our load."

In a few minutes, Dick and Dinah came down the street. Red Mule and Scrappie carried the boxes into the store and Miss Tyler checked the delivery. After they stacked the last one and Dick and Dinah were chewing a final apple, Red Mule and Scrappie saw Mace McDowell drive up to the curb on the other side of the street, where he parked his horse-and-mule truck. It was loaded with mules. They were packed into this truck like sardines in a box. Each mule tried to get his eyes up level with a crack so he could look from the covered truck bed. Mace went into The Dinner Bell. One of the mules who had his eyes level with one of the broad cracks in the truck bed looked over across the street and saw Dick and Dinah. Then he brayed and Dick and Dinah stopped pulling the jolt wagon. Dinah brayed back to him.

"Listen to that, won't you, Scrappie," Red

Mule said. "It breaks my heart to hear that piti-
ful mule talk. That's old Mace! He's stopped
at The Dinner Bell to get himself some coffee.
He'll be driving to Columbus tonight. He's taking that load to the cannery!"

"Can't Mace make a living some other way?"
Scrappie asked Red Mule.

"I've asked him that many times," Red Mule
said, with tears welling up in his eyes. "Think
of just going around and buying up mules and
trucking big loads like that one to the cannery!
I can count twelve on that truck, Scrappie!
Think of twelve mules from the little farms!"

Then another mule brayed from the truck
and old Dick answered him.

"That's a Lost Creek mule," Red Mule told
Scrappie. "He brays just a little different from
the Tiger River or the Sandee River mules.
Mules speak a different language on Lost Creek."

"Red Mule, you understand mule language
better than I do," Scrappie said.

"I'm older than you," he said. "You know
what that mule said to old Dick? He said,
'You're lucky.' And old Dick answered him,

'You bet we are.   We got good masters.'   That included you and me, Scrappie!"   Another mule spoke from the truck.   Dinah replied in a long, mournful tone.

"Where was he from and what did he say, Red Mule?"

"He's a Tiger River mule and he said to Dinah, 'We don't know where we're going.   We don't believe we're going to farms.   We might be going to the cannery!'   And old Dinah replied, 'Kick the slats off the truck.   Jump into the street.   Then run back to the green pastures! Escape before it is too late!' "

"Gee, Red Mule, you sure can understand mules."

"Just sit there and listen.   They'll all get to talking so loud here in a minute that Mace will have to leave his coffee and jump into his truck and drive it out of Blakesburg.   He's not supposed to park it there anyway.   But I'm glad he has.   Let other people hear the sad talk of those departing mules!   They don't want to leave here!"

Red Mule was right.   All the mules in the

truck wanted to talk at once. And Dick and Dinah tried to talk back. Mrs. Ezra Williams came down the street and she stopped and put her hands over her ears to stop the piercing sounds. She looked toward Red Mule, Scrappie, Dick, and Dinah and then she looked at the truckload of braying mules parked on Main Street. She went toward the mayor's office in a hurry with her hands over her ears.

"She's going to report that to the mayor," Red Mule shouted in Scrappie's ear. "Mace had better get away from The Dinner Bell while he can. His mules are talking too much. The mayor won't have all that mule talk in Blakesburg. It's too bad our mayor can't understand mule talk. If he could understand the things they are saying he'd have Mace locked up in jail."

Scrappie and Red Mule had to put their fingers in their ears to drown the sad sounds of twelve mules who were braying to Dick and Dinah. Mace got out of The Dinner Bell just as the mayor walked up the street. Mace jumped into his truck and drove down Main Street while his mules put their noses against the high truck bed

98

and wept. Dick and Dinah stood on their hind feet and pawed the air.

Scrappie and Red Mule still got jobs, but sometimes Scrappie was worried. I wonder if Dad hasn't been right all the time about mules, Scrappie thought the next Saturday morning as he lay awake in bed. Even if Red Mule and I love mules, they are still behind the times. Looking back to old times the way Red Mule does isn't enough. We've got to find something that mules can do better than machinery.

This was the day that Red Mule and Scrappie shared an order with the three tractor owners to haul twenty cords of driftwood to the Greenwood County Jail. Although he wouldn't admit it to anyone, Scrappie didn't think the mules had much of a chance. Today was the time the people of Blakesburg would see how much more wood the tractors could haul than the mules. If he and Red Mule got their share, they would get four of the twenty cords to haul. That would be four good loads up the Sandee River bank. But there would be Milford Royster, Jad Warnock, and Sylvester Lybrooks—all with their fast tractors. It would be a race, and how much chance did they have? Red Mule thought they would make out. He was going to use a big, young, and powerful span of mules, Sorrel Giant and Queen Lucy, to compete. He'd let good old Dick and Dinah rest on this day.

The Sandee River had flooded in winter and left piles of driftwood that the March and April suns had seasoned. Years ago Red Mule had started hauling driftwood to the people of Blakesburg to burn in fireplaces and stoves and to use for kindling. Hauling spring driftwood had been a profitable business for Red Mule and his team until Milford Royster, Jad Warnock, and Sylvester Lybrooks bought tractors and put them to work. Now they were sharing this business. Adam Linwood, Greenwood County jailor, gave the order each year to all four. The one who hauled the most on that day got the most pay. So each tried to haul more than his share.

This Saturday the tractor drivers began competing among themselves and overlooking Red Mule and Scrappie until suddenly something happened.   Milford got too close to Sandee River.   His tractor wheels started spinning and then sank down.   Jad tried to pull him out and his tractor stuck too.   Sylvester tried to pull Jad's tractor and he bogged down.

"Now we'll get the business," Red Mule told Scrappie while a crowd gathered on the river-bank and looked on and cheered for the mules. "Let 'em set there in the mud.   We won't stick. It's not neighborly, but trucks and tractors have never been good neighbors to mules."

Red Mule and Scrappie laid the driftwood on their jolt wagon.   They let the mules stay in their gait up the riverbank to the jailhouse and when they came back empty they let them run all the way.   They took load after load up the bank and raced back, thinking each time they'd have the tractors out when they returned.   Once Milford went up in Blakesburg and got Dave Attlebury's truck and hooked onto his tractor, but the truck wheels buried in the sand.

"Scrappie, they'll come to us this time," Red Mule said as they kept hauling.

Milford, Jad, and Sylvester worked most of

the day trying to get their tractors and Dave Attlebury's truck out. And all day Red Mule and Scrappie hauled driftwood. They let Sorrel Giant and Queen Lucy walk down the riverbank after the last load.

"Say, Red Mule," Milford said, walking over. "We're stuck. We're really stuck!"

"I see you are," Red Mule said, grinning.

"Do you suppose your mules could pull these tractors out?"

"Yes, but my mules are a little tired," Red Mule said. "We've had to put in three-fourths of that big order at the jail today. Sorrel Giant could pull one of the tractors out at a time if the singletree didn't break. Any mule I got will pull in water up to his belly. His engine won't choke! It won't bog down. It won't back-fire."

Milford looked down and shoved gravel around with his shoe.

"How much would you charge to pull our tractors and the truck out?" Milford asked, looking up quickly at Red Mule.

"It will be high," Red Mule said. "We'll

have to charge you by the foot, won't we, Scrappie?   About two bucks a foot will be right, don't you think, Scrappie?"

"You mean two dollars a foot?"   Milford said, his face getting red.

"That's the least we'll take," Scrappie replied.   "We've got pasture for our mules now. We've got hay in the barn to feed 'em this winter. We've got money to buy more mules."

"I won't pay that," Milford said.

"You'll have to have mules for that job," Red Mule told him.   "Heavy rains above and the water is rising.   No gasoline-pulled vehicle can pull you out of there.   Only the sure-footed, reliable mules can do it.   And I've got all the mules left around here.   It's all right with us, ain't it, Scrappie?   What about it, Sorrel Giant and Queen Lucy?"

Sorrel Giant and Queen Lucy walked on to get the last load.   Scrappie and Red Mule loaded the wood and were starting back when Milford came running over.

"We'll pay you that, Red Mule," he said. "I've talked to the boys.   We've agreed."

"The water is rising fast," he said excitedly. "Unhitch from your wagon and bring the mules. Maybe you can save us."

"Our Sorrel Giant and Queen Lucy will save your tractors," Red Mule said. "We'll be over soon as we can unhitch and get the drag chains from around the rough lock and the binding pole."

"Two dollars a foot!" Scrappie said. "More than fifty feet to pull each tractor and truck. That's over two hundred feet and it will be over four hundred dollars, Red Mule! Gee, that's money! That will save six, seven, or eight, maybe nine, more mules! They're dirt cheap now. Not anybody wants to buy a mule but us!"

More people in Blakesburg had heard about the tractors and truck being stuck in the soft sand at the water's edge. They knew it was rising now at a foot an hour. Many Blakesburg people came down to see if the river would get the truck and tractors. Among the crowd gathered on the riverbank was Scrappie's father. Bouncer and Mrs. Ezra Williams were among the crowd too.

When Red Mule backed the span of big mules into the river, Scrappie waded in and fastened the drag chain to the first tractor. Red Mule had to hold back with all his might on the lines. Then Scrappie told him to let them go. The giant mules bent low as they heaved forward with a great surge of power. They pulled the tractor slowly up to the dry riverbank. There was a great applause from the people for the mules when they did this.

"Our mules are showing them something, ain't they, Scrappie?" Red Mule whispered. "Now let's get the other two tractors and the truck!"

When they brought the second tractor out, a great shout went up. And when they pulled the third tractor out, the mules got a greater applause. Then came the real test of the mules' strength. The last was the two-ton truck, and water was up in the engine now. Red Mule backed the mules up to the truck. Scrappie fastened the chain. Dave Attlebury shifted his truck out of gear and sat at the steering wheel to guide it. The big mules got down and really pulled, an inch at a

time, until they pulled it from the muck.   This was the greatest display of mule strength the people in Blakesburg had ever seen.   A great applause—clapping of hands, whistles, screams, and shouts—went up!

After Red Mule had stepped off the distances, three feet for each step, Jad Warnock, Sylvester Lybrooks, Milford Royster, and Dave Attlebury walked up and paid him in cash.   For every step he had taken when he measured the distances his mules had pulled the tractors and truck, he got six dollars, two dollars for each foot.   They paid Red Mule in green folding money.   Scrappie had never seen Red Mule stuff so much folding money into his pockets before.   The people on the riverbank watched this too.   This was one time they had seen mules triumph over trucks and tractors!

Scrappie Finds a Way

Red Mule felt rich. "I knew we'd show them. Those tractors would be stuck in the mud yet if it wasn't for our mules. That was a fine sight, Scrappie, after all the bragging those fellows did, to see them sitting there helpless, having to beg us to pull them out of the mud."

Scrappie laughed. "Our mules did the job and none of the tractors could. We sure won." But then he thought, yes, we won, but only for a day. The mules have to eat every day. What are we going to do now? Plowing gardens and truck patches is over. All the work we have for our mules is to haul a few things from the railway station for Dad. Dad was right about mules. He knows what progress means. Milford Royster is pulling logs from the timber woods with his tractor. Jad Warnock is hauling gravel and sand from the river with his tractor. Sylvester Lybrooks is pulling a big cultivator with his tractor in the Sandee River bottoms. Red Mule and I don't have anything to do for our mules. We will soon have to go cut hay and store it to feed them this winter. Just as Dad said, tractors don't eat anything.

Scrappie walked inside the living room, where his father was sitting with his feet propped up, his paper on his lap. His father was asleep. Scrappie tiptoed over so he wouldn't wake him. He picked the paper up gently and sat down across from his father to read the sports page. He started turning to the sports page when suddenly he read a little headline: TURKEY IS USING OUR MULES. Then Scrappie forgot about the sports page.

He read in this small news item that the government had purchased several hundred mules to send to parts of the world where it would be most difficult to use mechanized equipment. Scrappie was so elated over finding this in the paper that he tore it out and put the clipping in his pocket. But the paper doesn't say who in our government is sending the mules to Turkey, he thought. Then, he took the clipping from his pocket and read it again. It definitely didn't say who was sending the mules.

Maybe mules are on their way back, Scrappie thought. If some use could only be found for mules, then our problem would be solved. Dad is right. We can't go on feeding our mules year after year and not have anything for them to do. But if we can only find a use for them, Red Mule will be sleeping in a feather bed and he'll have an account at the bank like he had when he was a young man. I can show Bouncer something. Then he won't be going around and saying that I smell like a mule and that he has to hold his nose every time he passes me.

Scrappie kept thinking about what he'd seen in the paper about the mules when he went upstairs to his room and to bed. He couldn't go to sleep for thinking about some place where mules could still be used. And he went to sleep thinking about it. He knew he had to write to somebody in the United States government to find out.

Next morning when Scrappie was awakened by his mother's tapping the ceiling below his bed with a broom handle, Scrappie had the answer. He knew what he was going to do. He was going to sit down after breakfast and write a letter to the President of the United States. If anybody knew a place for mules, he should be the one.

Blakesburg, Ky.

President of the United States,
White House,
Washington, D.C.

DEAR MISTER PRESIDENT:

We've got a problem down here and I thought you might be able to help us. I have a good friend and a partner in business by the name of Red Mule. Red Mule and I like mules and we try to save them from the canneries. There isn't enough work for mules here now that there are tractors.

Now I am Scrappie Lykins. I am twelve years old. I work with Red Mule except when I go to

112

school. When Red Mule gets gardens and truck patches to plow in Blakesburg, he does the plowing and I ride the disk and harrow the ground. Red Mule is too big to ride the disk harrow.

Mister President, is there any place where this country needs good mules? Don't you have something for mules that tractors and trucks can't do? Red Mule and I were having a hard time making enough to buy hay for these mules until Dad rented us pasture and then he gave us his meadows to cut on another farm. I'm helping pay for the mule pasture by working in my dad's store when there isn't any school and when Red Mule doesn't need me to help him on a job where we use a mule team. We cut the meadows, rake the hay, and haul it to the barn, and my father gives us half of the hay to feed our mules next winter.

Mister President, mules don't like to eat all the time. Mules like to work. So we must find something for our mules to do. Will you let us know if there is anything they can do that trucks and tractors can't?

Mister President, if you can think of anything let me know. Red Mule and I will appreciate it. The mules need help.

Very sincerely, your friend,

FRANK LYKINS, III

Through May and June and into July Scrappie and Red Mule mowed, raked, and hauled hay. Every day Scrappie's mother drove to the farm to see how Scrappie and Red Mule were coming along with the work. Often Frank Lykins left the store and drove out to the farm with his wife to see their son. Scrappie was bronzed because he worked bareheaded and without a shirt in the sun. The muscles in his arms and chest were tightening. The country life was good for him and his mother and father were as proud of the mules as Scrappie and Red Mule were.

Frank and Mary Lykins had found a new interest in their farm. It was more than an investment. Their son loved the farm and he had taught them to love it, too. They, for the first time, had seen the beauty in a hayfield. They had driven out in the afternoons about sunset while Scrappie and Red Mule were still working. They had stood and looked at the little shocks of golden-brown hay that Scrappie and Red Mule had mown and raked and stacked. Now these little stacks were ready to haul to the barn. All these golden haystacks in the last rays of a setting sun were a beautiful sight that excited Scrappie's parents.

By the middle of July, Red Mule and Scrappie had two barns filled and a third one was under way. One afternoon Scrappie's mother drove out and brought Scrappie a letter.

"Scrappie, this letter is from Washington, D.C.," she said. "It might be from the President."

Scrappie took the letter and opened it in a hurry. His eyes lit up like stars there in the bright July sunlight as he read.

"Oh, Mom, listen to this," he shouted. "Let me read it to you! It is from the President of the United States! He's answered my letter! He didn't forget to answer my letter! Gee, he must like mules!"

The White House
Washington, D.C.

Frank Lykins, III
Blakesburg, Kentucky

MY DEAR YOUNG FRIEND:

I am very happy to have your letter about mules. I realize you and Red Mule have a problem. Since I have been an Army man, I know mules have come in handy for the Army. They have carried troops and supplies over rough terrain and brought the wounded back. So I have referred your letter to the War Department. You can expect a man any day now, and certainly not later than September, to contact you about your mules.

In the meantime, I'll be thinking of other countries, and perhaps parts of our own country, which are undeveloped and where mules are needed. I agree with you, Scrappie; we don't want to lose our mules. We want them here for the next generation and the next and on and on. I believe there is a place in our civilization and in world civilization for the mule! He has occupied an important and useful place in the development of our great country. My young friend Scrappie, you can believe me, I'll do all I can to help you and Red Mule save the mules. We'll see if there isn't a place where we can use them. Thank you for writing me.

Very sincerely,
PRESIDENT OF THE UNITED STATES

"Gee, Mom, what about it!" Scrappie was very happy. "Here, take and keep this letter for me. Think of the President's writing me a letter! We mustn't tell Red Mule or Dad. But let this man come and surprise them!"

"I think it would be wonderful, Scrappie."

116

Then Scrappie went back to work shocking hay because Red Mule was raking up big windrows with the mule-drawn rake. His mother stood for a few minutes and watched his small brown arms move like pistons as he lifted forkfuls of bright, sweet-smelling hay into the stack.

One afternoon in early August when Scrappie and Red Mule were cutting an alfalfa meadow the third time, Scrappie's father and mother drove out to see hay in stacks on the meadow in the sunset. As they stood there another car drove over near the house where Scrappie and Red Mule lived. It stopped and a man got out and started walking toward the hayfield. He walked up to where Frank and Mary were standing.

"Can you tell me where I can find a boy by the name of Scrappie Lykins?" he said. "I inquired at a filling station in Blakesburg and I was directed out here."

He was a middle-aged man with graying temples and pink cheeks. He was wearing a tan suit and a soft gray hat. He smoked a cigar and carried a brief case.

117

"Sure, I can tell you where you can find him,"
Frank Lykins told him.   "That's the boy right

out there without a shirt and hat, who's as brown as a ripe raspberry.   He's my son!"

"Well, Mr. Lykins, I'm glad to know you," he said extending his hand.   "I'm Howard Riggerish.   I work for the United States government."

"And this is Mrs. Lykins, Scrappie's mother," Frank Lykins said, looking the stranger over.

"I suppose that letter your son wrote to the President of the United States made you very happy," Howard Riggerish told them.   "It really brought results."

"I didn't know my son wrote the President a letter," Frank Lykins said.   He was surprised. "I didn't know a thing about it!"

"Well, he did," Howard Riggerish said. "He wrote a letter asking the President what he could do to help him and somebody called Red Mule.   The letter was transferred to us.   So here I am.   Now, where is Red Mule?"

"That's Red Mule out there on that rake," Frank Lykins said.   "They're working to save hay for their mules this winter!"

"Would you mind calling both over here?"

Then Frank Lykins hollered for Scrappie to come over. And with a sweep of his hand he motioned for Red Mule to come.

When Scrappie walked up, his mother said, "Scrappie, this is Howard Riggerish."

"Glad to meet you," Scrappie said.

"And this is Red Mule," Frank Lykins said as Howard Riggerish looked big Red Mule over from head to foot.

"Very glad to know you, Red Mule," he said.

"The same to you." Red Mule sighed as he looked back across the big meadow of sun-cured alfalfa, which was very pretty in the sunset. "Say, that's a pretty field of hay, ain't it!"

"What are you fellows going to feed that pretty hay to?" Howard Riggerish asked.

"Mules," Scrappie said. "We've got thirty-seven mules, and before the end of this month we'll have fifty."

"That's my business here," Howard Riggerish said. "Scrappie, that letter you wrote the President brought results!"

"Shucks, Scrappie, did you write the President?" Red Mule asked.

"Sure did," Scrappie replied.

"I've come to look over your mules," Howard Riggerish told them. "We pay top prices for strong, healthy mules between the ages of three and six!"

"All of ours but two, Dick and Dinah, are between three and six," Red Mule said. "And Dick and Dinah are not for sale anyway. Not one of our mules has a blemish on him. They are as sound as silver dollars."

"If your mules are sound and young, as you say, I'll take all of them," Howard Riggerish said. "And I'll take a lot more when you buy them up and let me know."

"Say, what do you know about this," Frank Lykins said. His face was beaming. "Scrappie, how come you ever thought to write the President?"

"Well, I read something in a newspaper one evening about the United States sending mules to Turkey," Scrappie explained. "But the paper didn't say who was in charge of the buying. So I wrote to the top man of the United States to find out!"

121

"Scrappie, I didn't think you'd know to do that," Red Mule said, grinning until he showed his big teeth. "You're smarter than I thought you was. But I always thought you'd do something for mules!"

Scrappie's face lit up with joy. He was happy and his mother was happy too. She looked at her son and smiled.

"I'll take a shipment of mules this month," Howard Riggerish said. "I'm staying at the Central Hotel in Blakesburg and I'd like to see your mules tomorrow! Later I'll buy as many as you can get and put in good condition. The government has plans for mules in a number of countries."

"Gee," Scrappie said. "Where'll we find 'em?"

"Boys, that's business," Frank Lykins said as he pulled his son over close and put his arm around his neck. "Scrappie, you and your partner have licked this mule problem. You've found something they can do. You've got the problem whipped!"

"Red Mule, you'll be sleeping on a feather bed again," Scrappie said.

"We've got to save more mules first," Red Mule said. "Then we can talk about sleep."

Then Red Mule grinned broadly as Scrappie had seen him do the day when he threw the clods up into the elm leaves. He showed all of his big teeth behind his long red beard. Scrappie smiled too as the August evening wind blew across the meadow and tousled his long, uncombed hair. Dick and Dinah pawed the meadow dirt with their forefeet and Dick brayed.

"Dick's telling me to come back to 'em, Mr. Riggerish," Red Mule said. "We'll see you in the morning and show you our mules. Right now I must get back to Dick and Dinah."

About the Author and Artist

Red Mule is Jesse Stuart's third book for children. It was preceded by the popular *The Beatinest Boy* and *A Penny's Worth of Character*, which, like his many books for grownups, earned the highest critical praise throughout the country. He has won many awards, prizes, and fellowships.

He was born in W-Hollow near Riverton, Kentucky, where he still lives, and went to a one-room Kentucky school. After graduating from high school, he worked his way through college, and then did graduate work at Vanderbilt University and Peabody College.

At seventeen he started teaching in a rural schoolhouse, and he eventually became superintendent of various city and county schools in Kentucky.

Robert G. Henneberger is a distinguished young artist who has already won great acclaim for his illustrations in *The Beatinest Boy*, *A Penny's Worth of Character*, and many other children's publications. Born in Baltimore, he grew up more interested in drawing pictures than in other childhood activities. After the war he graduated from Rhode Island School of Design, settled in Providence with his wife, and started his career as an illustrator.